THE LEGEND OF THE KIWI

Retold and Illustrated by Lyn Kriegler

Alister Taylor
The Old Post Office
Martinborough
A DOROTHY BUTLER BOOK

IN the very early days of New Zealand, Tane, the God of the Forest, made friends with all the birds. From time to time he would gather them together to address them, and teach them wisdom. He taught Huia how to search with her long, curved beak for the delicious Huhu grub; he showed Moa how to find good nesting places in the swamps, and where to look for tasty Matai seeds. Bellbird learned, in time, to search out the sweetest, nectar-bearing bush flowers.

To all the birds Tane taught music, that they might fill the forest with glorious song.

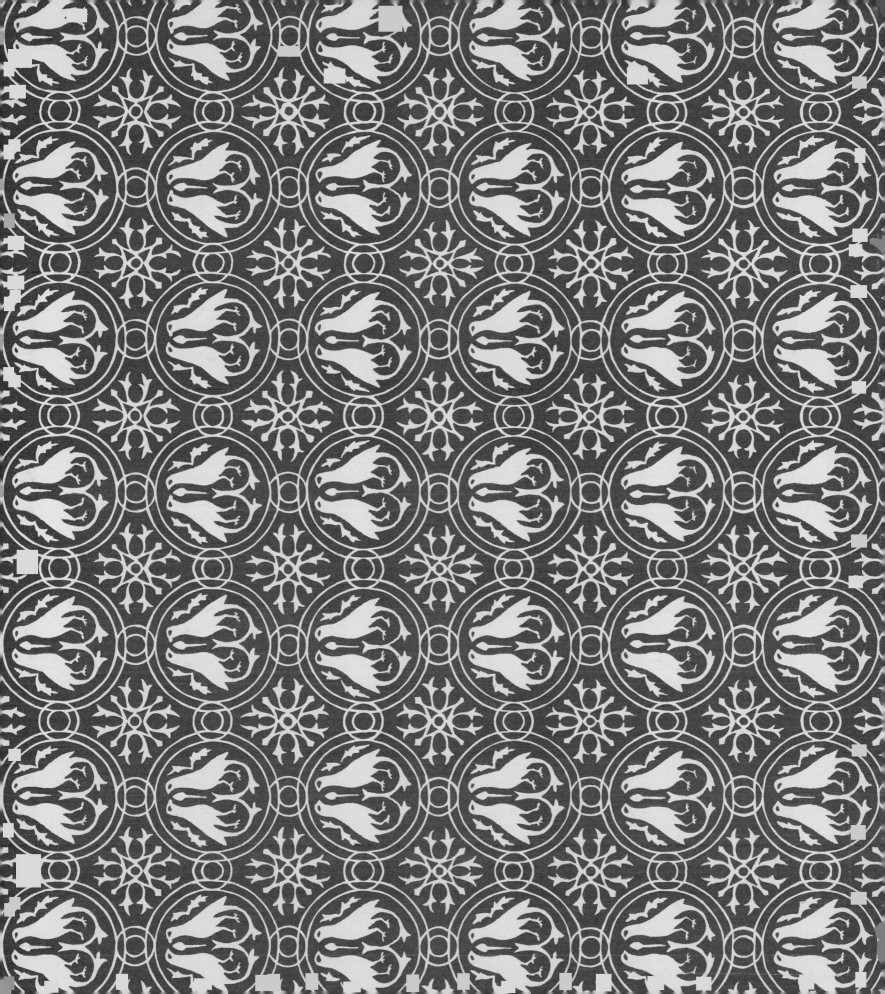

To Dandu, Andrew and Edward

The Legend of the Kiwi.
Retold and illustrated by Lyn Kriegler.
Text and illustrations © 1981 Lyn Kriegler.
First published 1981 by Alister Taylor Publishers,
The Old Post Office, Martinborough, New Zealand.
All rights reserved. This book is copyright and no
part may be published or transmitted in any form
whatsoever without prior permission, in writing, from
the publisher.

Design by Lyn Kriegler and Tom Elliott.
Script lettering by Tom Elliott.
Endpapers by Lyn Kriegler.
Type set in Granjon
by Jacobson Typesetters Ltd, Auckland.
Printed in Japan
by Kyodo Printing Company Limited

Alister Taylor Publishers Children's Book Division.
Director Deborah Coddington.
Editor Dorothy Butler.

ISBN 0-908578-27-X

NOW in those days Kiwi could fly. Joyously he spread his wings, swooping and diving, coasting and soaring in the brilliant sunshine. Gaily he sang and joked with the other birds as together they enjoyed the bountiful fruits of the forest: juicy berries and golden nectar, tasty insects, and tender shoots and leaves.

IN time, however, Kiwi began spending more and more time feasting in the trees. He was gradually becoming too fat and lazy to sing, too stuffed and sleepy to fly with the other birds.

As the sunny days slipped by, Kiwi spent less and less time hopping from branch to branch.

"There is just as much food on the ground as in the trees", he thought. Soon he was spending all of his time on the forest floor, eating and sleeping.

THEN, one day Kiwi saw some delicious insects hovering just above his head.

"I shall fly and snap them up at once!" he thought.

But try as he might, he could not rise from the ground. His wings had become useless.

EFORE long, the other birds noticed his growing laziness. Gone was his sleek, swift shape. And where was his song? Out-of-tune belches had replaced his pure, joyful notes.

Kiwi, in turn, felt the growing disapproval of the other birds. More and more, he hid himself from sight in the undergrowth.

NOW it came to pass that one day Tane called a great gathering of the birds. All answered except Kiwi. Tane sent scouts in all directions, calling him by name, but without success. Kiwi was hidden deep in his secret place under the roots of a Puriri tree. Although he heard the summons, he was too frightened to show himself. Whenever the messengers came near, he crouched even lower.

IN the end, Tane called for the hunt to cease, and the meeting to begin. But he was very angry. He charged all the birds present to seek out Kiwi wherever they went. When they found him, they were to tell him of Tane's wrath, and demand that he present himself and ask for forgiveness.

KIWI is weak-hearted and cowardly!" screamed Kea as he searched the steep and rocky ledges of the snow-clad alpine peaks.

"No longer does he brave wind and cloud, rejoicing in his strength! Shamefaced he cowers before our Lord Tane. In fear he hides himself from his brothers! Who cares to know him now?"

"**K**IWI is ugly and graceless!" cried Heron as she searched among the scented reeds and the fern-clad banks of lake and stream.

"Idle he sits, while his belly grows fat and his neck grows thick. Who cares to know him now?"

"KIWI is dull and witless!" trilled Tui as he searched the flowering treetops and the sunlit shadows of the forest floor. "No more does he warble and sing; no longer does he make clever conversation! Who cares to know him now?"

COWERING in his secret place, Kiwi heard their cries, and trembled.

Terrified he crouched, closing his ears to their calls, trying to forget Tane's threat of punishment.

When night fell and the other birds were asleep, he slipped out. Nervously, he scratched grubs from the forest floor. In fear, he ferreted out worms with his sensitive beak. He was so hungry!

TIME passed, and Kiwi forgot his days of delight and daring among the branches and in the wide sky. He became a bird of the night, a dweller of dark and mysterious places where the bright eyes of the other birds would never again behold him.

In time, he regained his happiness; but the joy of free and soaring flight was never again to be his. To this day, the Kiwi is a hidden bird, rejecting the bright light of day, and cherishing the soft darkness of his chosen world.

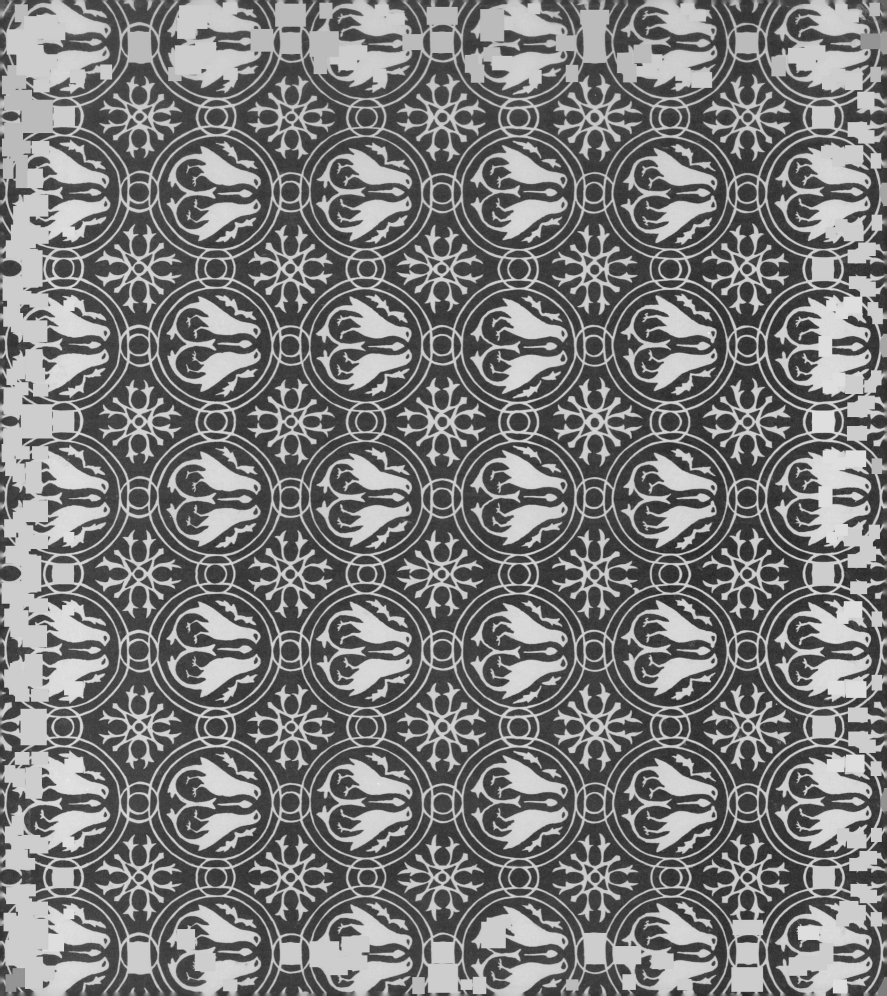